SUICIDE CHAPEL

BY

SEABURY QUINN

British Library Cataloguing-in-Publication Data
A catalogue record for this book is available from the
British Library

CONTENTS

SEABURY QUINN

Seabury Grandin Quinn was born in Washington D.C. in 1889. In 1910, he graduated from law school, and was admitted to the District of Columbia Bar. He served in World War I, and after his Army service became editor of a group of trade papers in New York. His first published work was 'The Law of the Movies' (1917), in *The Motion Picture Magazine*, and his first published fictional story was 'Demons of the Night' (1918), in *Detective Story Magazine*. He introduced the occult detective Jules de Grandin as a character in 1925, and continued writing tales about him until 1951. Quinn's stories were incredibly popular, and between the twenties and fifties he appeared in *Weird Tales* magazine more times than both Robert E. Howard and H. P. Lovecraft. His novel *Roads* was also widely read. Quinn died in old age on Christmas Eve.

SUICIDE CHAPEL

Although the calendar declared it was late May the elements and the thermometer denied it. All day the rain had streamed torrentially and the wind keened like a moaning banshee through the newly budded leaves that furred the maple boughs. Now the raving tempest laid a lacquer-like veneer of driven water on the window-pane and howled a bawdy chanson down the chimney where a four-log fire was blazing on the hearth. Fresh from a steaming shower and smelling most agreeably of Roman Hyacinth, Jules de Grandin sat before the fire and gazed with unconcealed approval at the toe tip of his purple leather slipper. A mauve silk scarf was knotted Ascot fashion round his throat, his hands were drawn up in the sleeves of his deep violet brocade dressing-gown, and on his face was that look of somnolent content which well-fed tom-cats wear when they are thoroughly at peace with themselves and the world. "Not for a thousand gold Napoléons would I set foot outside this house again tonight," he told me as he dipped into the pocket of his robe, fished out a pack of "Marylands" and set one of the evil-smelling things alight. "Three times, three separate, distinct times, have I been soaked to saturation in this *sacré* rain today. Now, if the Empress Josephine came to me in the flesh and begged that I should go with her, I would refuse the assignation. Regretfully, *mais certainement*, but definitely. Me, I would not stir outside the door for—"

"Sergeant Costello, if ye plaze, sor," came the rich Irish brogue of Nora McGinnis, my household factotum, who appeared outside the study entrance like a figure materialised in a vaudeville illusion. "He says it's most important, sor."

"*Tiens*, bid him enter, *ma petite*, and bring a bottle of the Irish whiskey from the cellar," de Grandin answered with a smile; then:

"*C'est véritablement toi, ami?*" he asked as the big Irishman came in and held cold-reddened fingers to the fire. "What evil wind has blown you out on such a fetid night?"

"Evil is th' word, sor," Costello answered as he drained the glass de Grandin proffered. "Have ye been radin' in th' papers of th' Gogswell gur-rl's disappearin', I dunno?'

"But yes, of course. Was she not the young woman who evaporated from her dormitory at the Shelton School three months ago? You have found her, *mon vieux*? You are to be congratulated. In my experience—

"Would yer experience tell ye what to do when a second

gur-rl pops outa sight in pracizely th' same manner, lavin' nayther hide nor hair o' clue?"

De Grandin's small blue eyes closed quickly, then opened wide, for all the world like an astonished cat's. "But surely, there is some little trace of evidence, some hint of hidden romance, some—"

"Some nothin' at all, sor. Three months ago today th' Gogswell gur-rl went to 'er room immejiately afther class. Th' elevator boy who took her up seen her walk down th' hall, two classmates said hello to her. Then she shut her door, an' shut herself outa th' wor-rld entirely, so it seems. Nobody's seen or heard o' her since then. This afthernoon, just afther four o'clock, th' Lefètre gur-rl comes from th' lab'ratory, goes straight to 'er room an'"—he paused and raised his massive shoulders in a ponderous shrug—"there's another missin'-persons case fer me to wrastle wid. I've come to ask yer help, sor."

De Grandin pursed his lips and arched his narrow brows. "I am not interested in criminal investigation, *mon sergent*."

"Not even to save an old pal in a hot spot, sor?"

"*Hein?* How is it you say?"

" 'Tis this way, sor. When th' Cogswell gur-rl evaporated, as ye say, they gave th' case to me, though be rights it b'longed to th' Missin' Persons Bureau. Well, sor, when a gur-rl fades out that way there may be anny number o' good reasons fer it, but mostly it's because she wants to. An' th' more ye asks th' family questions th' less ye learn. 'Had she anny love affairs?' sez you, an' 'No!' sez they, as if ye'd been set on insultin' her. 'Wuz she happy in her home?' ye asks, an' 'Certainly, she wuz!' they tells ye, an' they imply ye've hinted that they bate her up each night at eight o'clock an' matinees at two-fifteen. So it goes. Each time ye try to git some reason for her disappearin' act they gits huffier till finally they sez they're bein' persecuted, an' ye git th' wor-rks, both from th' chief an' newspapers."

"Perfectly," de Grandin nodded. "As Monsieur Gilbert says, a policeman's life is not a happy one."

"Ye're tellin' me! But this time it's still worse, sor. When I couldn't break th' Cogswell case they hinted I wuz slowin' down, an' had maybe seen me best days. Now they goes an' dumps this here new case in me lap an' tells me if I fail to break it I'll be back in harness wid a nightsthick in me hand before I've checked another birthday off. So, sor, if ye could—"

"*Pas possible!* They dare say this to you, the peerless officer, the pride of the *gendarmerie*—"

"They sure did, sor. An' lots more—'

"Aside, Friend Trowbridge; aside *mon sergent*—make passageway for me. Await while I put on my outside clothing. I shall show them, me. We shall see if they can do such things to my tried friend—*les crétins!*"

So incredibly short was the interval elapsing before he rejoined us with his hat pulled down above his eyes, trench coat buttoned tight beneath his chin, that I could not understand until I caught a flash of violet silk pyjama leg bloused out above the top of his laced boots.

"Lead on, my *sergent*," he commanded. "Take us to the place which this so foolish girl selected for her disappearance. We shall find her or otherwise!"

"Would ye be manin' 'or else', sor, I dunno?"

"*Ah bah*, who cares? Let us be about our task!"

"Sure, we got a full description o' th' clothes she wore when she skedaddled," Costello told us as we drove out towards the fashionable suburb where the Shelton School was located. "She wuz wearin' orange-coloured lounging pyjamas an' pegged orange-coloured slippers."

"Pegged?" de Grandin echoed. "Was she then poor—"

"Divil a bit o' it, sor. Her folks is rich as creases, but she wuz overdrawn on her allowance, and had to cut th' corners till her next cheque came."

"One comprehends. And then—"

"There ain't no then, sor. We've inventoried all her wardrobe an' everything is present but th' duds she wore when she came in from class. Not even a hat's missin'. O'

7

course, that don't mean nothin' much. If she'd set her heart on lammin', she coulda had another outfit waitin' for her somewheres else, but—"

"Quite but, my friend," de Grandin nodded. "Until the contrary appears, we must assume she went away *sans trousseau.*"

With characteristic fickleness the shrewish storm had blown itself away while we drove from the city, and a pale half-waning moon tossed like a bit of lucent jetsam in a purling surf of broken clouds as we drew up beneath the porte-cochère of the big red brick dormitory whence Emerline Lefètre had set forth for her unknown goal six hours earlier.

"Yas, suh," replied the coloured elevator operator, visibly enjoying the distinction of being questioned by the police. "Ah remembers pufficly erbout hit all. Miss Lefètre come in from lab. She seemed lak she was in a powerful hurry, an' didn't say a thing, 'ceptin' to thank me for de letters."

"The letters? Do you by any happy circumstance remember whence they came?"

"Naw, suh. Ah don' look at de young ladies' mail, 'ceptin' to see who hit's for. I recolleck dese letters mos' partickler, though, 'cause one of 'em wuz smelled up so grand."

"Perfumed?"

"An' how, suh. Jus' lak de scents de conjur doctors sell, on'y more pretty-smellin'. Dat one wuz in a big vanilla envelope. All sealed up, it wuz, but de odour come right through de paper lak hit wuz nothin' a-tall."

"*Merci bien.* Now, if you will kindly take us up—"

The little room where Emerline Lefètre dwelt was neat and colourless as only hospital, barrack or dormitory rooms can be. No trace of dust marred imitation mahogany furniture. Indifferent reproductions of several of the less rowdy Directoire prints were ranged with mathematical precision on the walls. The counterpane was squared with blocks of blue and white so virginally chaste as to seem positively spinsterish. "*Mon Dieu*, it is a dungeon, nothing less," de Grandin murmured as he scanned the place. "Can anybody blame a girl for seeking sanctuary from such terrible surround—*quel parfum horrible!*" His narrow nostrils quivered as he sniffed the air. "She had atrocious taste in scent, this so mysteriously absent one."

"Perhaps it's the elegant perfume the elevator operator mentioned." I ventured. "He'd have admired something redolent of musk—"

"*Dis donc!* You put your finger on the pulse, my friend! It is the musk. But yes. I did not recognise him instantly, but now I do. The letter she received was steeped in musk. Why, in Satan's name? one wonders."

9

Thoughtfully, he walked slowly to the window, opened it and thrust his head out. looking down upon the cement walk some fifty feet below. Neither ivy, water-spout nor protuberance of the building offered foothold for a mouse upon the flat straight wall.

"I do not think she went that way," he murmured as he turned to look up at the overhanging roof.

"Nor that way, either, sor," Costello rejoined, pointing to the overhanging of mansard roof some seven feet above the window-top.

"U'm? One wonders." Reaching out, de Grandin tapped an iron cleat set in the wall midway of the window's height. From the spike's tip branched a flange of a turnbuckle, evidently intended to secure a shutter at some former time. "A very active person might ascend or—*parbleu!*"

Breaking off his words half uttered, he took a jeweller's loop out of his raincoat pocket, fixed it in his eye, then played the beam of his electric torch upon the window-sill, subjecting it to a methodical inspection.

"What do you make of this, my friends?" he asked as he passed the glass to us in turn, directing his light ray along the grey stone sill and indicating several tiny scratches on the slate. "They may be recent, they may have been here since the building was erected," he admitted as we handed back the glass, "but in cases such as this there are no such things as trifles."

Once more he leant across the window-sill, then mounted it and bent out till his eyes were level with the rusty iron cleat set in the wall.

"*Morbleu*, it is a repetition!" he exclaimed as he rejoined us. "Up, my *sergent*, up, friend Trowbridge, and see what you can see upon that iron."

Gingerly, I clambered to the sill and viewed the rusty cleat through the enlarging-glass while Costello played the flashlight's beam upon it. On the iron's reddish surface, invisible, or nearly so, to naked eyes, but clearly visible through the loop's lens, there showed a row of sharp, light scratches, exactly duplicating those upon the window-sill.

"Bedad, I don't know what it's all about, sor," Costello rumbled as he concluded his inspection, "but if its' a wild-goose chase we're on I'm thinkin' that we've found a feather in th' wind to guide us."

"*Exactement*. One is permitted to indulge that hope. Now let us mount the roof.

"Have the care," he cautioned as Costello took his ankles in a firm grip and slid him gently down the slanting, still-wet slates. "I have led a somewhat sinful life, and have no wish to be projected into the beyond without sufficient time to make my peace with heaven."

"No fear, sor," grinned Costello. "Ye're a little pip squeak, savin' yer presence, an' I can swing ye be th' heels till mornin' if this rotten brickwor-rk don't give way wid me."

Wriggling eel-like on his stomach, de Grandin searched the roof slates inch by careful inch from the leaded gutter running round the roof bank's lower edge to the lower brick ridge that marked the incline's top. His small blue eyes were shining brightly as he rejoined us.

"*Mes amis*, there is the mystery here." he announced solemnly. "Across the gutter to the slates, and up the slates until the roof's flat top is reached, there is a trail of well defined, light scratches. Moreover, they are different."

"Different, sor? How d'ye mean—"

"Like this: Upon the window-sill they are perceptibly more wide and deep at their beginning than their end—like exclamation marks viewed from above. In the gutter and upon the roof they are reversed, with deeper gashes at the lower ends and lighter scratches at their upper terminals."

"O.K., sor. Spill it. I'm not much good at riddles."

A momentary frown inscribed twin upright wrinkles between de Grandin's brows. "One cannot say with surety, but one may guess," he answered slowly, speaking more to himself than to us. "If the marks were uniform one might infer someone had crawled out of the window, mounted to the gutter by the ringbolt set into the wall, then climbed upon the roof. An active person might accomplish it. But the situation is quite otherwise. The scratches on the slates reverse the scorings on the window-sill."

"You've waded out beyond me depth, now, sor," Costello answered.

"*Tiens*, mine also," the Frenchman grinned. "But let us hazard a conjecture: Suppose one wearing hobnailed boots—or shoes which had been pegged, as Miss Lefètre's were—had crawled out from this window: how would he use his feet?"

"To stand on, I praysume, sor."

"*Ah bah*. You vex me, you annoy me, you get upon my goat! Standing on the sill and reaching up and out to grasp that iron cleat, he would have used his feet to brace himself and pivot on. His tendency would be to turn upon his toes, thereby tracing arcs or semicircles in the stone with the nails set in his shoes. But that is not the case here. The scorings marked into the stone are deeper at beginning, showing that the hobnailed shoes were scratching in resistance, clawing if you please, against some force which bore the wearer of those shoes across the window-sill. Digging deeply at beginning, the nail marks taper off, as the shoes slipped from the stone and their wearer's weight was lifted from the sill.

'When we view the iron cleat we are upon less certain ground. One cannot say just how a person stepping to the iron would move his feet in climbing to the roof; but when we come to read the slates we find another chapter in this so puzzling story. Those marks were left by someone who fought not to mount the roof; but who was struggling backwards with the strength of desperation, yet who was steadily forced upwards. Consider, if you please: The fact that such resistance, if successful, would have resulted in this person's being catapulted to the cement path and almost surely killed, shows us conclusively the maker of those marks regarded death as preferable to going up that roof. Why? one asks."

"Pardon me, sir, are you from headquarters?" Slightly nasal but not at all unmusical, the challenge drawled at us across the corridor. From the doorway of the room set opposite to Emerline's a girl regarded us with one of the most indolent, provocative "come-hither" looks I'd ever seen a women wear. She was of medium height, not slender and not stout, but lushly built, with bright hair, blonde as a well-beaten egg, worn in a page-boy bob and curled up slightly at the ends. From round throat to high white insteps she was draped in black velvet pyjamas which had obviously not been purchased ready-made, but sculptured to her perfect measure, for her high, firm, ample breasts pushed up so strongly underneath the velvet that the dip of the fabric to her flat stomach was entirely without wrinkles. Her trousers were so loose about the legs they simulated a wide skirt, but at the hips they fitted with a skin-tight snugness as revealing as a rubber bathing-suit. From high-arched carefully pencilled brows to blood-red toenails she was the perfect figure of the siren, and I heard Costello gasp with almost awe-struck admiration as his eyes swept over her.

"We are, indeed, *ma belle*," de Grandin answered. "You wish to speak with us?"

Her blue eyes widened suddenly, then dropped a veil of carefully mascaraed lashes which like an odalisque's thin gossamer revealed more than it hid. They were strange eyes to see in such a young face, meaningful and knowing, a little weary, more than a little mocking. "Yes," she drawled lazily. "You're on the case of Emerline Lefètre, aren't you?"

"Yes, *Mademoiselle*."

"Well, I'm sure she disappeared at five o'clock."

"Indeed? How is it that you place the time?"

A shrug which was a slow contortion raised her black-draped shoulders and pressed the pointed breasts more tightly still against her tucked-in jacket. "I was in bed all afternoon with a neuralgic headache. The last lab period today was out at half past four, and I heard the girls come down the hall from class. There's not much time till dinner when we come in late from lab, and a warning bell rings in the dorm at three minutes before five. When it went off this afternoon it almost split my head apart. The rain had

15

stopped; at least I didn't hear it beating on my window, but the storm had made it dark as midnight, and at first I thought it was a dream. Then I heard some of the girls go hurrying by, and knew that it was five o'clock, or not more than a minute past. I was lying there, trying to find energy to totter to the bureau for some mentholated cologne, when I heard a funny noise across the hall. I'm sure it came from Emerline's room."

"A funny noise, *Mademoiselle!* How do you mean?"

A little wrinkle furrowed down the smooth white skin between the pencilled brows. "As nearly as I can describe it, it was like the opening quaver of a screech owl's cry, but it was shut off almost as it started. Then I heard a sound of stamping, as though there were a scuffle going on in there. I s'pose I should have risen and investigated, but I was too sick and miserable to do more than lie there wondering about it. Presently I fell asleep and forget about it till I heard you in her room just now." She paused and patted back a yawn. "Mind if I go in and have a look around?" she asked, walking towards us with a swinging, aphrodisiacally undulating gait. The aura of a heavy, penetrating perfume—musk-based patchouli essence, I determined at a hasty breath—seemed hovering round her like a cumulus of tangible vapour.

As far as Jules de Grandin was concerned her blandishments might have been directed at a granite statue. "It is utterly forbidden, *Mademoiselle*. We are most grateful for your help, but until we have the opportunity to sweep the place for clues we request that no one enter it."

"What d'ye mean, sweep th' place for clues, sor?" asked Costello as we drove towards home.

"Precisely what I said, *mon vieux*. There may be clues among the very dust to make this so mysterious puzzle clear."

Arrived at the house, he rummaged in the broom cupboard, finally emerging with my newest vacuum sweeper underneath his arm. It was a cleaner I had let myself be argued into buying because, as the young salesman pointed out, instead of a cloth bag it had a sack of oiled paper which when filled could be detached and thrown away. To my mind this had much merit, but Nora McGinnis begged to disagree, and so the old cloth-bellows sweeper was in daily use while the newer, sanitary engine rested in the closet.

"Behold, my friend," he grinned, "there is a virtue to be found in everything. Madame Nora has refused to use the sweeper, thereby making it impossible for you to get return on your investment, but her stubbornness assists me greatly, for here I have a pack of clean fresh paper bags in which to gather up our evidence, You comprehend?"

"Ye mean ye're goin' to vaccum-sweep that room out to th' Shelton School?" Costello asked incredulously.

"Perfectly, my friend. The floor, the walls, perhaps the ceiling. When Jules de Grandin seeks for clues he does not play. Oh, no."

The door of Emerline Lefètre's room was open on a crack as we marched down the corridor equipped with vacuum sweeper and paper refills, and as de Grandin thrust it open with his foot we caught the heavy, almost overpowering odour of patchouli mixed with musk.

"*Dame!*" de Grandin swore. "She has been here, *cette éroto-furieuse*, against my express orders. And she has raised the window, too. How can we say what valuable bit of evidence has been blown out—*morbleu!*"

Positively venomous with rage, he had stamped across the room to slam the window down, but before he lowered it had leant across the sill. Now he rested hands upon the slate and gazed down at the cement pavement fifty feet below, a look of mingled pain and wonder on his face.

"Trowbridge, Costello, *mes amis*, come quickly!" he commanded, beckoning us imperiously. "Look down and tell me what it is you see."

Spotlighted by a patch of moonlight on the dull-grey cement walk a huddled body lay, inert, grotesque, unnatural-looking as a marionette whose wires have been cut. The flash of yellow hair and pale white skin against the sombre elegance of sable velvet gave it positive identification.

18

"How th' divil did she come to take that tumble?" Costello asked as we dashed down the stairs, disdaining to wait on the slowly moving elevator.

"*Le bon Dieu* and the devil only know," de Grandin answered as he knelt beside the crumbled remnant of the girl's bright personality and laid a hand beneath her generously swelling breast.

The impact of her fall must have been devastating. Beneath her crown of gold-blonde hair her skull vault had been mashed as though it were an eggshell; through the skin above her left eye showed a staring splinter of white bone where the shattered temporal had pierced the skin; just above the round neck of her velvet jacket thrust a jagged chisel-edge of white, remnant of a broken cervical vertebra. Already purple bruises of extravasated blood were forming on her face; her left leg thrust out awkwardly, almost perpendicularly to her body's axis, and where the loose-legged trouser had turned back we saw the Z-twist of a compound comminutive fracture.

"Is she—" began Costello, and de Grandin nodded as he rose.

"Indubitably," he returned. "Dead like a herring."

"But why should she had jumped?" I wondered. "Some evil influence—a wild desire to emulate—"

He made a gesture of negation. "How far is it from here to

19

the house wall?" he asked.

"Why, some eighteen feet, I judge."

"*Précisément.* That much, at least. Is it in your mind her fall's trajectory would have been so wide an arc?"

"What's that?"

"Simply this, by blue! Had she leaped or fallen from the window she should have struck the earth much nearer to the building's base. The distance separating ground and window is too small to account for her striking thus far out; besides it is unlikely that she would have dived head first. Men sometimes make such suicidal leaps, women scarcely ever. Yet all the evidence discloses that she struck upon her head; at least she fell face forward. "Why?"

"You imply that she was—"

"I am not sure, but from the facts as we observe them I believe that she was thrown, and thrown by one who had uncommon strength. She was a heavy girl; no ordinary person could have lifted her and thrown her through a window, yet someone must have done just that; there is no evidence of struggle in the room."

"Shall I take charge, sor?" asked Costello.

De Grandin nodded. "It will expedite our work if you will be so kind. When she is taken to the morgue I wish you would prevent the autopsy until I have a chance to make a more minute inspection of the body. Meantime I have important duties elsewhere."

Methodically, as though he'd been a janitor—but with far more care for detail—he moved the vacuum sweeper back and forth across the floor of the small tragic room, drew out the paper bag and sealed and labelled it. Then with a fresh bag in the bellows he swept the bed, the couch, the draperies. Satisfied that every latent trace of dust had been removed, he shut the current off, and, his precious bags beneath his arm, led the march towards my waiting car.

A sheet of clean white paper spread across the surgery table made background for the miscellany of fine refuse which he emptied from the sweeper's bags. Microscope to eye, he passed a glass rod vigorously rubbed with silk back and forth across the dust heap. Attracted by the static charge fine bits of rubbish adhered to the rod and were subjected to his scrutiny. As he completed his examination I viewed the salvage through a second microscope, but found it utterly uninteresting. It was the usual hodgepodge to be culled by vacuuming a broom-cleaned room. Tiny bits of paper, too fine to yield to straw brooms' pressure, little flecks of nondescript black dust, a wisp or two of wool fibre from the cheap rug, the trash was valueless from any viewpoint, as far as I could see.

"*Que diable?*" With eyes intently narrowed he was looking at some object clinging to his glass rod.

"What is it?" I demanded, leaning closer.

"See if you can classify it," he returned, moving aside to let me look down through the viewhole of the microscope.

It was a strand of hair three-quarters of an inch or so in length, curled slightly, like a human body hair, but thicker, coarser in its texture. Reddish rusty brown at tip, it shaded to a dull grey at the centre and bleached to white transparency about the base. I saw it was smooth-scaled upon its outer surface and terminated in a point, showing it had never been cut or, if clipped, had sufficient time to grow to its full length again.

"Let us proceed," I heard him whisper as he moved his polished rod again across the heap of sweepings. "Perhaps we shall discover something else."

Slowly he moved the rod across the furrowed edges of the dust heap, pausing now and then to view a fresh find. A splinter of straw, a tiny tag of paper, fine, powdered dust, these comprised his salvage, till: "Ah?" he murmured, "ah-ha?" Adhering to the rod there was another wisp of hair, almost the counterpart of his first find, except it was more nearly uniform in colour, dull lack-lustre rust all over, like an aged tom-cat's fur, or the hair of some misguided woman who has sought a simulation of her vanished youth by having her grey tresses dyed with henna.

"What—" I began, but he waved me silent with a nervous

gesture as he continued fishing with his rod. At last he laid the rod aside and began to winnow the dust piles through a fine wire screen. Half an hour's patient work resulted in the salvaging of two or three small chocolate-coloured flakes which looked for all the world like grains of bran and when held close to our noses on a sheet of folded paper gave off a sweetly penetrating odour.

"You recognise them?" he asked.

"Not by sight. By their smell I'd say they contained musk."

"Quite, yes," he nodded. "They are musk. Crude musk, such as the makers of perfumery use."

"But what should that be doing in a young girl's room—"

"One wonders with the wonder of amazement. One also wonders what those hairs did there. I should say the musk flakes were contained in the brown envelope the elevator boy delivered to Mademoiselle Lefètre. As for the hairs—"

The tinkle of the telephone broke off his explanation. "Yes, my *sergent*, it is I," I heard him answer. "He is? Restrain him—forcefully, if necessary. I shall make the haste to join you.

"Come, let us hurry," he commanded as he set the phone down.

"Where, at this hour o' night, for pity's sake?"

"Why, to the morgue, of course. Parnell, the coroner's physician, insists on making an autopsy on the body of Miss Henrietta Sidlo within the hour. We must look at her first."

"Who the devil was Miss Henrietta Sidlo?" I asked as we commenced our hurried journey to the city morgue.

"The so attractive blonde young woman who was killed because she could not mind her business and keep from the room we had forbidden her to enter."

"What makes you so sure she was killed? She might have fallen from the window, or—"

"Or?" he echoed.

"Oh, nothing. I just had a thought."

"I rejoice to hear it. What was it, if you please?"

"Perhaps she thought as you did, that Miss Lefètre had climbed to the roof, and tried to emulate the feat experimentally."

I had expected him to scout my theory, but he nodded thoughtfully. "It may be so," he answered. "It seems incredible that one should be so foolish, but the Sidlo girl was nothing if not unbelievable, *n'est-ce-pas?*"

Beneath the searing glare that flooded from the clustered arclights set above the concave operating-table in the morgue's autopsy room her body showed almost as pale as the white tiles that floored and walled the place. She had bled freely from the nose and ears when skull and brain were smashed at once, and the dried blood stained her chin and cheeks and throat. De Grandin took a spray-nosed hose and played its threadlike stream across her face and neck, sponging off the dried blood with a wad of cotton. At length: "What is it that you see?" he asked.

Where the blood and grime had washed away were five light livid patches, one some three inches in size and roughly square, and extending from it four parallel lines almost completely circling the neck. At the end of each was a deeply pitted scar, as if the talons of some predatory beast had sunk into the flesh.

"Good heavens," I exclaimed; "it's terrible!"

"But naturally. One does not look for beauty in the morgue. I asked you what you saw, not for your *impression esthétique*."

I hesitated for a breath and felt his small blue eyes upon me in a fixed, unwinking stare, quizzical, sardonic; almost, it seemed, a little pleading. Long years ago, when we had known each other but a day, he and I had stood beside another corpse in this same morgue, the corpse of a young girl who had been choked and mauled to death by a gorilla. "Sarah Humphreys—" I began; and:

"*Bravo, bravissimo!*" he whispered. "You have right, my friend. See, here is the bruise left by the heel of his hand; these encircling marks, they are his fingers; these jagged, deep-set marks the wounds left by his broken nails. Yes, it is so. There is no thumb print, for he does not grasp like men, he does not use his thumb for fulcrum."

"Then those hairs you found when you swept up the room—"

"*Précisément.* I recognised them instantly, but could not imagine how they came there. If—one moment, if you please!"

Bending quickly he took the dead girl's pale plump hands in his and with his penknife tip skimmed underneath the rims of her elaborately lacquered nails, dropping the salvage into a fresh envelope. "I think that we shall find corroboration in a microscopic test of these," he stated, but the bustling entrance of the coroner's physician cut him short.

"What's going on here?" Doctor Parnell asked. "No one should touch this body till I've finished my examination—"

"We do but make it ready for you, *cher collègue*," de Grandin answered with fictitious mildness as he turned away. Outside he muttered as we climbed into my car: "There are fools, colossal fools, damned fools, and then there is Parnell. He is superlative among all fools, friend Trowbridge."

Three-quarters of an hour later we put the scrapings from the dead girl's nails beneath a microscope. Most of the matter was sheer waste, but broken and wedged firmly in a tiny drop of nail stain we came upon the thing we sought, a tiny fragment of gorilla hair.

"*Tiens*, she fought for life with nature's weapons, *cette pauvre*," he murmured as he rose from the examination. "It is a pity she should die so young and beautiful. We must take vengeance for her death, my friend."

Amber brocade curtains had been drawn against the unseasonably chilly weather and a bright fire crackled on the hearth of the high-mantelled fireplace of the lounging-room of the Lefètre home in Nyack. Harold Lefètre greeted us restrainedly. Since dinnertime the day before he had been interviewed by a succession of policemen and reporters, and his nerves and patience were stretched almost to the snapping-point.

"There isn't anything that I can add to what you've been already told," he said like one who speaks a well-learned piece. "Emerline was just past seventeen, she had no love affairs, wasn't especially interested in boys. Her scholastic standing was quite good, though she seldom got past B grades. She was not particularly studious, so it couldn't have been a nervous breakdown forced by overstudy. She stood well enough in marks not to have been worried over passing her examinations; she was happy in her home. There is no reason, no earthly reason I can think of, for her to disappear. I've told you everything I know. Suppose you try looking for her instead of quizzing me."

Costello's face flushed brick-red. He had been against the interview, expecting a rebuke would be forthcoming.

De Grandin seemed oblivious to Lefêtre's censure. His eyes were travelling round the charming room in a quick, stock-taking gaze. He noted with approval the expensive furniture, the bizarre small tables with their litter of inconsequential trifles, cinnabar and silver cigarette-containers, fashionable magazines, bridge markers, the deep bookshelves right and left of the big fireplace, the blurred blues and mulberries of the antique china in the un-glassed cabinets. In a far, unlighted corner of the room his questing glance seemed resting, as though he had attained the object of his search. In apposition to the modern, western, super-civilised sophistication of the other bric-à-brac the group of curios seemed utterly incongruous; a hippopotamus leg with hoof intact, brass-lined to form a cane stand and holding in its tube a sheaf of African assagais. Above the group of relics hung a little drum no bigger than a sectioned coconut, with a slackly tensioned head of dull grey parchment. "*Monsieur*," the Frenchman suddenly demanded, "you were in Africa with Willis Cogswell in 1922?"

Lefêtre eyed him sharply. "What has that to do—"

"It was Monsieur Cogswell's daughter who vanished without trace three months ago, *n'est-ce-pas?*"

"I still don't see—"

"There were three members of your African adventure, were there not: yourself, and Messieurs Cogswell and Everton?"

Anger flamed in our host's face as he turned on Costello. "What has all this got to do with Emerline's case?" he almost roared. "First you come badgering me with senseless questions about her, now you bring this 'expert' here to pry into my private life—"

"You did not part with Monsieur Everton in friendship?" de Grandin broke in imperturbably. Then, as if his question were rhetorical: "But no. Quite otherwise. You and he and Monsieur Cogswell quarrelled. He left you vowing vengeance—"

"See here, I've had enough of this unwarranted—"

"And ninety days ago he struck at Willis Cogswell through the dearest thing that he possessed. Attend me very carefully, *Monsieur*. You have heard that shock caused Monsieur Cogswell to collapse, that he died of a heart seizure two days following his daughter's disappearance—"

"Of course, he did. Why shouldn't he? He'd been suffering from angina for a year, had to give up business and spend half his time in bed. His doctor'd warned him anything exciting might prove fatal—"

"*Précisément.* He fell dead in his library. His butler found him dead upon the floor—"

"That's true, but what—"

De Grandin drew a slip of folded paper from his pocket. "This was in your friend's hand when the butler found him," he answered as he held the missive towards our host. It was a piece of coarse brown paper, torn, apparently from a grocery bag, and pencilled on it in black chalk was one word: *Bokoli*.

The anger faded from Lefètre's face; fear drained his colour, left him grey.

"You recognise the writing?" asked de Grandin.

"No, no, it can't be," Lefètre faltered. "Everton is dead— we—I saw him—"

"And these, *Monsieur*, we found among the sweepings from your daughter's room," de Grandin interrupted. "You recognise them, *hein?*" Fixed with adhesive gum to a card of plain white paper, he extended the gorilla hairs we'd found the night before.

Utter panic replaced fear in our host's face. His eyes were glassy, bright and dilated as if drugged with belladonna. They shifted here and there, as though he sought some channel of escape. His lips began to twist convulsively.

"This—this is a trick!" he mumbled, and we saw the spittle drooling from the corners of his mouth. "This couldn't be—"

His hands shook in a nervous frenzy, clawing at his collar. Then suddenly his knees seemed softening under him, and every bit of stiffness left his body so that he fell down in a heap before the hearth, the impact of his fall rattling the brass tools by the fireplace.

Involuntarily I shivered. Something evil and soft-footed seemed to shuffle in that quiet room, but there was no seeing it, no hearing it, no way of knowing what it was; only the uncanny, hideous feel of it—clammy, cold, obscenely leering.

"Now—so!" de Grandin soothed as he lowered his flask from the reviving man's lips. "That's better, *n'est-ce-pas?*"

He helped Lefètre to a chair, and, "Would it not be well to tell us all about it?" he suggested. "You have had a seething pot inside you many years, *Monsieur*; it has boiled, then simmered down, then boiled again, and it has brought much scum up in the process. Let us skim it off, *comme ça*"—he made a gesture as if with a spoon—"and throw it out. Only so shall we arrive at mental peace."

Lefètre set his face like one who contemplates a dive in icy water. "There were four of us on safari through Bokoliland," he answered; "Cogswell, his wife Lysbeth, a Boer settler's daughter, Everton and I. We'd found the going pretty rough; no ivory, no trading fit to mention, no gold, and our supplies were running low. When we reached Shamboko's village the men were all out hunting, but the women and old men were kind to us and fed and lodged us. In normal circumstances we'd have waited there until the chief came back and tried to do some trading, but on the second evening Everton came hurrying to our hut half drunken with excitement.

" 'I've just been to the Ju-Ju house,' he told me. 'D'ye know what they've got there? Gold! Great heaps and stacks o' yellow dust, enough to fill out hats and pockets, and a stack o' yellow diamonds bigger than your head. Let's go!'

"Now, the Bokoli are a fairly peaceful folk, and they'd take a lot from white men, but if you monkey with their women or their Ju-Ju you'd better have your life insurance premiums all paid. I'd seen the body of a man they'd 'chopped' for sacrilege one time, and it had put the fear o' God in me. They'd flayed the skin off him, not enough to kill him, but the torment must have been almost past standing. Then they'd smeared honey on the raw nerve ends and staked him down spread-eagled in a clearing in the jungle. The ants had found him there—millions of the little red ones—and they'd cleaned the flesh off his bones as if they had been boiled.

"I wasn't having any of that, so I turned the proposition down, but the others were all for it. Finally I yielded and we sneaked down to the Ju-Ju house. It was just as Everton had said. The gold was piled in little pyramidal heaps before the idol in a semi-circle, with the diamonds stacked up in the centre. The offerings must have been accumulating over several centuries, for there's little gold in the Bokoli country, and no diamonds nearer than five hundred miles. But there the stuff was, ready for our taking.

"We stuffed our haversacks and pockets and set out for the coast within an hour, anxious to put as many miles as possible between us and the village before the medicine man paid his morning visit to the Ju-Ju and found out what we'd done.

"Everton began to act queer from the start. He'd sneak away from camp at night and be gone hours at a time without an explanation. One night I followed him. He made straight for a clearing by the river and sat down on the grass as if waiting for someone. Presently I saw a shadow slipping from the bush and next moment a full-grown gorilla shambled out into the moonlight. Instead of rushing Everton the monster stopped a little distance off and looked at him, and Everton looked back, then—think I'm a liar if you wish—they *talked* to one another. Don't ask me how they did it; I don't know. I only know that Everton addressed a series of deep grunts to the great beast and it answered him in kind. Then they parted and I trailed him back to camp.

"Three days later the Bokoli caught us. We'd just completed dinner and were sitting down to smoke when all at once the jungle seemed alive with 'em, great strapping blacks with four-foot throwing-spears and bullhide shields and vulture feathers in their hair. They weren't noisy about it. That was the worst of it. They appeared like shadows out of nowhere and stood there in a ring, just looking at us. Old Chief Shamboko did the honours, and he was as polite about it as the villain in a play. No reproaches for the diamonds and the gold dust we'd made off with, though they must have represented his tribe's savings for a century or more. Oh, no, he put it squarely to us on the ground of sacrilege. The Ju-Ju was insulted. He'd lost face. Only blood could wash away the memory of the insult, but he'd be satisfied with one of us. Just one. We were to make the choice. Then he walked back to the ring of warriors and stood waiting for us to announce which one of us would go back to be flayed alive and eaten up by ants. Pretty fix to be in, eh?"

"You made no offer to return the loot?" de Grandin asked.

"I'll say we did. Told him he might have our whole trade stock to boot, but he wasn't interested. The treasure we had taken from the temple had been tainted by our touch, so couldn't be put back, and only things dug from the earth were suitable as offerings to the Ju-Ju, so our trade stuff had no value. Besides, they wanted blood, and blood was what they meant to have."

"One sees. Accordingly—?"

"We tossed for it. Lysbeth, Conroy's wife, drew out a coin and whispered something to her husband. Then he and

Everton and I stood by as she flipped it. Conroy beat us to the call and shouted 'Heads!' And heads it came. That left Everton and me to try.

"He shouted 'Tails!' almost before the silver left her hand. It came up heads again, and I was safe."

"And so—"

"Just so. The Bokoli couldn't understand our words, of course, but they knew that Everton had lost by his demeanour, and they were on him in a second, pinioning his arms against his sides with grass rope before he had a chance to draw his gun and shoot himself.

"Considering what he was headed for, you could hardly blame him, but it seemed degrading, the way he begged for life. We'd seen him in a dozen desperate fixes when his chance of coming through alive seemed absolutely nil, but he seemed like another person, now, pleading with us to shoot him, or die fighting for him, making us the most outlandish offers, promising to be our slave and work for ever without wages if we'd only save him from the savages. Even old Shamboko seemed to feel embarrassed at the sight of such abysmal cowardice in a white man, and he'd ordered his young men to drag their victim off when Everton chanced to kick the silver coin which sent him to his fate. The florin shone and twinkled in the moonlight when he turned it over. Then he and I and all of us realised. It was a trick piece Lysbeth used, an old Dutch florin with two heads. There hadn't been a chance her man could lose the toss, for she'd told him to call heads, and she'd flipped the coin herself, so none of us could see it was a cheat.

"Everton turned sober in a second. Rage calmed him where his self-respect was powerless to overcome his fear of torture, and he rose with dignity to march away between the loki warriors. But just before he disappeared with them into the bush he turned on us. 'You'll never know a moment's safety, any of you,' he bellowed. 'The shadow of the jungle will be on you always, and it'll take the dearest things you have. Remember, you'll each lose the thing you love most dearly.'

"That was all. The Boloki marched him off, and we never saw him again."

"But, *Monsieur*—"

"But two weeks later, when we were almost at the outskirts of the Boer country, I woke up in the night with the sound of screaming in my ears. Conroy lay face downwards by the campfire, and just disappearing in the bush was a great silver-backed gorilla with Lysbeth struggled in his arms."

"You pursued—"

"Not right away. I was too flabbergasted to do more than gape at what I saw for several seconds, and the big ape and the woman were gone almost before you could say 'knife'.

Then there was Conroy to look after. He'd had a dreadful beating, though I don't suppose the beast had more than merely flung him from his way. They're incredibly powerful, those great apes. Conroy had a dislocated shoulder and two broken ribs, and for a while I thought he'd not pull through. I pulled his shoulder back in place and bandaged him as best I could, but it was several weeks before he regained strength to travel, and even then we had to take it slowly.

"I kept us alive by hunting, and one day while I was gunning I found Lysbeth. It was a week since she'd been stolen, but apparently she'd never been more than a mile or so away, for her body hung up in a tree-fork less than an hour's walk from camp, and was still warm when I found it.

"The ape had ripped her clothing off as he might have peeled a fruit, and apparently he'd been none too gentle in the process, for she was overlaid with scratches like a net. Those were just play marks, though. It wasn't till he tired of her—or till she tried to run away—he really used his strength on her. Down her arms and up her thighs were terrible great gashes, deep enough to show the bone where skin and flesh had been shorn through in places. Her face was beaten absolutely flat, nose, lips and chin all smashed down to a bloody level. Her neck was broken. Her head hung down as if suspended by a string, and on her throat were bruise marks and the nail-prints of the great beast's hands where he had squeezed her neck until her spinal column snapped. I"—Lefètre faltered and we saw the shadow of abysmal horror flit across his face—"I don't like to think what had happened to the poor girl in the week between her kidnapping and killing."

Costello looked from our host to de Grandin. " 'Tis a highly interesting' tale, sor," he assured the Frenchman, "but I can't say as I sees where it fits in. This here now Everton is dead—ain't he?" he turned to Lefètre.

"I've always thought—I like to think he is."

"Ye saw 'im march off wid th' savages, didn't ye? They're willing' workers wid th' knife, if what ye say is true."

De Grandin almost closed his eyes and murmured softly, like one who speaks a poem learned in childhood and more than half forgotten: "It was December 2,1923, that Lieutenant José Garcia of the Royal Spanish Army went with a file of native troops to inspect the little outpost of Akaar, which lies close by Bokoliland. He found the place in mourning, crazed with sorrow, fear and consternation. Some days before a flock of fierce gorillas had swept down upon the village, murdered several of the men and made away with numerous young women. From what the native told him, Lieutenant Garcia learned such things had happened almost for a year in the Bokoli country, and that the village of the chief Shamboko had been utterly destroyed by a herd of giant apes—" "That's it!" Lefètre shrieked. "We've never known. We heard about the ape raids and that Shamboko's village had been wrecked by them, but whether they destroyed it before Everton was put to death or whether they came down on it in vengeance—Conroy and I both thought he had been killed, but we couldn't know. When his daughter disappeared I didn't connect it with Africa, but that paper Conroy clutched when he dropped dead, those hairs you found in Emerline's room—"

"*Exactement*," de Grandin nodded as Lefètre's voice trailed off. "Perfectly, exactly, quite so, *Monsieur*. It is a very large, impressive 'but'. We do not know, we cannot surely say, but we can damn suspect."

"But for th' love o' mud, sor, how'd this here felly git so chummy wid th' apes?" Costello asked. "I've seen some monkeys in th' zoo that seemed to have more sense than many a human, but—"

"You don't ask much about companions' former lives in Africa," Lefètre interrupted, "but from scraps of information he let drop I gathered Everton had been an animal trainer in his younger days and that he'd also been on expeditions to West Africa and Borneo to collect apes for zoos and circuses. It may be he had some affinity for them. I know he seemed to speak to and to understand that great ape in the jungle— d'ye suppose—"

"I do, indeed, *Monsieur*," de Grandin interrupted earnestly. "I am convinced of it."

"Sure, it's th' nuttiest business I iver heard of, sor," Costello declared as we drove home. " 'Tis wild enough when he stharts tellin' us about a man that talks to a gorilly, but when it's intaymated that a ape clomb up th' buildin' an' sthold th' gur-rl—"

"Such things have happened, *mon ami*," de Grandin answered. "The records of the Spanish army, as well as reports of explorers, vouch for such kidnappings—"

"O.K., sor; O.K. But why should th' gorillies choose th' very gur-rls this felly Everton desired to have sthold? Th' apes ye tell about just snatch a woman—any woman—that chances in their way, but these here now gorillies took th' very—"

"*Restez tranquil*," de Grandin ordered. "I would think, I desire to cogitate. *Nom d'un porc vert*, I would meditate, consider, speculate, if you will let me have a little silence!"

"Sure, sor, I'll be afther givin' ye all ye want. I wuz only—"

"Nature strikes her balance with nicety," de Grandin murmured as though musing aloud. "Every living creature pays for what he has. Man lacks great strength, but reinforces frailty with reason; the bloodhound cannot see great distances, but his sense of smell is very keen; nocturnal creatures like the bat and owl have eyes attuned to semi-darkness. What is the gorilla's balance? He has great strength, a marvellous agility, keen sight, but—*parbleu*, he lacks the sense of smell the lesser creatures have! You comprehend?"

"No, sor, I do not."

"But it is simple. His nose is little keener than his human cousins', but even his flat snout can recognise the pungent scent of crude musk at considerable distance. We do not know, we cannot surely say the Cogswell girl received an envelope containing musk upon the night she disappeared. We know that Mademoiselle Lefètre did." Abruptly:

"What sort of day was it Miss Cogswell disappeared?" he asked Costello.

The Irishman considered for a moment; then: "It wuz a wet, warm day in March, much like yesterday," he answered.

"It must have been," de Grandin nodded. "The great apes are susceptible to colds; to risk one in our northern winter out of doors would be to sign his death warrant, and this one was required for a second job of work."

Costello looked at him incredulously. "I s'pose ye know how old th' snatchin' monkey wuz?" he asked ironically.

"Approximately, yes. Like man, gorillas grey with age, but unlike us, their grey hairs show upon their backs and shoulders. A 'silverback' gorilla may be very aged, or he may still be in the vigour of his strength. They mature fully at the age of fourteen; at twenty they are very old. I think the ape we seek is something like fifteen years old; young enough to be in his full prime, old enough to have been caught in early youth and trained consistently to recognise the scent of musk and carry off the woman who exuded it."

"Th' tellyphone's been ringin' for a hour," Nora McGinnis told us as we drew up at my door. " 'Tis a Misther Lefètre, an' he wants ye to call back—"

"*Merci bien,*" de Grandin called as he raced down the hall and seized the instrument. In a moment he was back. "Quick, at once, right away, my friends," he cried. "We must go back to Nyack."

"But, glory be, we've just come down from there," Costello started to object, but the look of fierce excitement in the Frenchman's face cut his protest short.

"Monsieur Lefètre has received a note like that which killed his friend Cogswell," de Grandin announced. "It was thrust beneath his door five minutes after we had gone."

"And this," de Grandin tapped the scrap of ragged paper, "this shall be the means of trapping him who persecutes young girls."

"Arrah, sor, how ye're goin' to find 'im through that thing is more than I can see," Costello wondered. "Even if it has his fingerprints upon it, where do we go first?"

"To the office of the sheriff."

"Excuse me, sor, did ye say th' sheriff?"

"Your hearing is impeccable, my friend. Does not *Monsieur le Shérif* keep those sad-faced, thoughtful-looking dogs, the bloodhounds?"

"Be gob, sor, sure he does, but how'll ye know which way to lead 'em to take up th' scent?"

De Grandin flashed his quick, infectious grin at him. "Let us consider local geography. Our assumption is the miscreant we seek maintains an ape to do his bidding. Twice in three months a young girl has been kidnapped from the Shelton School—by this gorilla, we assume. America is a wondrous land. Things which would be marvels otherwise pass unnoticed here, but a gorilla in the country is still sufficiently a novelty to excite comment. Therefore, the one we seek desires privacy. He lives obscurely, shielded from his neighbours' prying gaze. Gorillas are equipped to walk, but not for long. The aerial pathways of the trees are nature's high road for them. *Alors*, this one lives in wooded country. Furthermore, he must live fairly near the Shelton School, since his ape must be able to go there without exciting comment, and bring his quarry to his lair unseen. You see? It is quite simple. Somewhere within a mile or so of Shelton is a patch of densely wooded land. When we have found that place we set out hounds upon the track of him whose scent is on this *sacré* piece of paper, and—*voilà!*"

"Be gorry, sor, ye'll have no trohble findin' land to fit yer bill," Costello assured him. "Th' pine woods grow right to th' Shelton campus on three sides, an' th' bay is on th' other."

The gentle bloodhounds wagged their tails and rubbed their velvet muzzles on de Grandin's faultlessly creased trousers. "Down, noble ones," he bade, dropping a morsel of raw liver to them. "Down, canine noblemen, peerless scenters-out of evil doers. We have a task to do tonight, thou and I."

He held the crudely lettered scrap of paper out to them and bade them sniff it, then began to lead them in an ever-widening circle through the thick-grown pine trees. Now and then they whimpered hopefully, their sadly thoughtful eyes upon him, then put their noses to the ground again. Suddenly one of them threw back his head and gave utterance to a short, sharp, joyous bark, followed by a deep-toned, belling bay.

"*Tallis au!*" de Grandin cried. "The chase is on, my friends. See to your weapons. What we seek is fiercer than a lion or a bear, and more stealthy than a panther."

Through bramble-bristling thicket, creeping under low-swung boughs and climbing over fallen trees, we trailed the dogs, deeper, deeper, ever deeper into the pine forest growing in its virgin vigour on the curving bay shore. It seem to me we were an hour on the way, but probably we had not followed our four-footed guides for more than twenty minutes when the leprous white of weather-blasted clapboards loomed before us through the wind-bent boughs. "Good Lord," I murmured as I recognised the place. "It's Suicide Chapel!"

"Eh? How is it you say?" de Grandin shot back.

"That's what the youngsters used to call it. Years ago it was the meeting-place of an obscure cult, a sort of combination of the Holy Rollers and the Whitests. They believed the dead are in a conscious state, and to prove their tenets their pastors and several members of the flock committed suicide *en masse*, offering themselves as voluntary sacrifices. The police dispersed the congregation, and as far as I know the place has not been tenanted for forty years. It has an evil reputation, haunted, and all that, you know."

"*Tenez*, I damn think it is haunted now by something worse than any of the old ones' spooks," he whispered.

The ruined church was grim in aspect as a Dorè etching. In the uncertain light of an ascending moon its clapboard sides, almost nude of paint, seemed glowing with unearthly phosphorescence. Patches of blue shadow lay like spilled ink on the weed-grown clearing round the edifice; the night wind keened a mournful threnody in the pine boughs. As we scrambled from the thicket of scrub evergreen and paused a moment in reconnaissance the ghostly hoot of an owl echoed weirdly through the gloom.

De Grandin cradled his short-barrelled rifle in the crook of his left arm and pointed to the tottering, broken-sided steeple. "He is there if he is here," he announced.

"I don't think that I follow ye," Costello whispered back. "D'ye mane he's here or there?"

"Both. The wounded snake or rodent seeks the nearest burrow. The cat things seek the shelter of the thickets. The monkey folk take to the heights when they are hunted. If he has heard the hounds bay he has doubtlessly done the same—*mor-dieu!*"

Something heavy, monstrous, smotheringly bulky, dropped on me with devastating force. Hot, noisome breath was in my face and on my neck, great, steel-strong hands were clutching at my legs, thick, club-like fingers closed around my arms, gripping them until I thought my biceps would be torn loose from my bones. My useless gun fell clattering from my hands, the monster's bristling hair thrust in my eyes, my nose, my mouth, choking and sickening me as I fought futilely against his overpowering strength. Half fainting with revulsion I struggled in the great ape's grasp and fell sprawling to the ground, trying ineffectively to brace myself against the certainty of being torn to piece. I felt my head seized in a giant paw, raised till I thought my neck would snap, then bumped against the ground with thunderous force. A lurid burst of light blazed in my eyes, followed by a deafening roar. Twice more the thunderous detonations sounded, and as the third report reverberated I felt the heavy weight on top of me go static. Though the hairy chest still bore me down, there was no movement in the great encircling arms, and the vice-like hands and feet had ceased their torturing pressure on my arms and legs. A sudden sticky warmness flooded over me, wetting through my jacket and trickling down my face.

"Trowbridge, *mon vieux, mon brave, mon véritable ami*, are you alive, do you survive?" de Grandin called as he and Costello hauled the massive simian corpse off me. "I should have shot him still more quickly, but my trigger finger would not mind my brain's command."

"I'm quite alive," I answered as I got unsteadily upon my feet and stretched my arms and legs tentatively. "Pretty well mauled and shaken, but—"

"*S-s-sh*," warned de Graindin. "There is another we must deal with. *Holà l'haut!*" he called. "Will you come forth, *Monsieur*, or do we deal with you as we dealt with your pet?"

Stark desolation reigned within the ruined church. Floors sagged uncertainly and groaned protestingly beneath our feet; the cheap pine pews were cracked and broken, fallen in upon themselves; throughout the place the musty, faintly acrid smell of rotting wood hung dank and heavy, like miasmic vapours of a marsh in autumn. Another smell was noticeable, too; the ammonia-laden scent of pent-up animals, such as hovers in the air of prisons, lazarets and primate houses at the zoo.

Guided by the odour and the searching beam shot by de Grandin's flashlight, we crossed the sagging floor with cautious steps until we reached the little eminence where in the former days the pulpit stood. There, like the obscene parody of a tabernacle, stood a great chest, some eight feet square, constructed of stout rough-sawn planks and barred across the front with iron uprights. a small dishpan half filled with water and the litter of melon rinds told us this had been the prison of the dead gorilla.

De Grandin stooped and looked inside the cage. "*Le pauvre sauvage*," he murmured. "It was in this pen he dwelt. It was inhuman—*pardieu!*" Bending quickly he retrieved a shred of orange satin. He raised it to his nose, then passed it to us. It was redolent of musk.

"So, then, Jules de Grandin is the fool, the *imbécile*, the simpleton, the ninny, the chaser-after-shadows, *hein?*" he demanded. "Come, let us follow through our quest."

"Th' place seems empty, sor," Costello said as, following the wall, we worked our way towards the building's front. "If there wuz anny body here—Howly Mither!"

Across our parth, like a doll cast aside by a peevish child

there lay a grotesque object. The breath stopped in my throat, for the thing was gruesomely suggestive of a human body, but as de Grandin played his flashlight on it we saw it was a life-sized dummy of a woman. It was some five feet tall, the head was decorated by a blonde bobbed wig, and it was clothed in well-made sports clothes—knit pullover, a kilted skirt of rough tweed, Shetland socks, tan heelless shoes—the sort of costume worn by eight in ten high school and college girls. As we bent to look at it the cloyingly sweet scent of musk assailed our nostrils.

"Is not all plain?—does it not leap to meet the eye?" de Grandin asked. "This was the implement of training. That hairy one out yonder had been trained for years to seek and bring back this musk-scented dummy. When he was letter-perfect in discovering and bringing back this lifeless simulacrum, his master sent him to the harder task of seeking out and stealing living girls who had the scent of musk upon them. *Ha*, one can see it plainly—the great ape leaping through the shadowed trees, scaling the school roof as easily as you or I could walk the streets, sniffing, searching, playing at this game of hide-and-seek he had been taught. Then from the open window comes the perfume which shall tell him that his quest is finished; there in the lighted room he sees the animated version of the dummy he had learned to seize and carry to this *sacré* place. He enters. There is a

49

scream of terror from his victim. His great hand closes on her throat and her cry dies out before it is half uttered; then through the treetops he comes to the chapel of the suicides, and underneath his arm there is—*morbleu*, and what in Satan's name is that?"

As he lectured us he swung his flashlight in an arc, and as it pointed towards the ladder-hole that led up to the ruined belfry its darting ray picked up another form which lay half bathed in shadows, like a drowned body at the water's edge.

It was—or had been—a man, but it lay across our path as awkwardly as the first dummy. Its arms and legs protruded at unnatural angles from its trunk, and though it lay breast down the head was turned completely round so that the face looked up, and I went sick with disgust as I looked on what had once been human features, but were now so battered, flattened and blood-smeared that only staring, bulging eyes and broken teeth protruding through smashed lips told life had once pulsed underneath the hideous, shattered mask. Close beside one of the open, flaccid hands a heavy whip-stock lay, the sort of whip that animal trainers use to cow their savage pupils. A foot or so of plaited rawhide lash frayed from the weighted stock, for the long, cruel whip of braided leather had been ripped and pulled apart as though it had been made of thread.

"God rest 'is sinful soul!" Costello groaned. "Th' gorilly

musta turned on 'im an' smashed 'im to a pulp. Looks like he'd tried to make a getaway, an' got pulled down from them stheps, sor, don't it?"

"By blue, it does; it most indubitably does," de Grandin agreed. "He was a cruel one, this, but the whip he used to beat his ape into submission was powerless at the last. One can find it in his heart to understand the monster's anger and desire for revenge. But pity for this one? *Non!* He was deserving of his fate, I damn think."

"All th' same, sor—Howly Saint Patrick, what's that?" Almost overhead, so faint and weak as to be scarcely audible, there sounded a weak, whimpering moan.

"Up, up, my friends, it may be that we are in time to save her!" the little Frenchman cried, leaping up the palsied ladder like a seaman swarming up the ratlines.

We followed him as best we could and halted at the nest of crossbeams marking the old belfry. For a moment we stood silent, then simultaneously flashed our torches. The little spears of light stabbed through the shrouding darkness for a moment, and picked up a splash of brilliant orange in the opening where the bell had hung. Lashed to the bell-wheel was a girl's slim form, arms and feet drawn back and tied with cruel knots to the spokes, her body bowed back in an arc against the wheel's periphery. Her weight had drawn the wooden cycle down so that she hung dead-centre at its bottom, but the fresh, strong rope spliced to the wheel-crank bore tesimony to the torment she had been subjected to, the whirling-swinging torture of the medieval bullwheel.

"Oh, please—please kill me!" she besought as the converging light beams played upon her pain-racked face. "Don't swing me any more—I can't—stand—" her pleas trailed off in a thin whimpering mewl and her head fell forward.

"Courage, *Mademoiselle*," the small Frenchman comforted. "We are come to take you home."

"But no, *mon sergent*," Jules de Grandin shook his head in deprecation as he watched the ice cube slowly melting in his highball glass, "I have a great appreciation of myself, and am not at all averse to advertising, but in this case I must be anonymous. You it was who did it all, who figured out the African connection, and who found the hideaway to which the so unfortunate Miss Lefètre was conveyed. Friend Trowbridge and I did but go along to give you help; the credit must be yours. We shall show those fools down at headquarters if you are past your prime. We shall show them if you are unfit for crime detection. This case will make your reputation firm, and that you also found what happened to the Gogswell girl will add materially to your fame. Is it not so?"

"I only wish to God I did know what happened to poor

Margaret Cogswell," the big detective answered.

De Grandin's smiling face went serious. "I have the fear that her fate was the same as that of Monsieur Cogswell's first wife. You recall how she was mauled to death by a gorilla? I should not be surprised if that ten-times-cursed Everton gave the poor girl to his great ape for sport when he had tired of torturing her. Tomorrow you would be advised to take a squad of diggers to that chapel of the suicides and have them search for her remains. I doubt not you will find them."

"An' would ye tell me one thing more, sor?"

"A hundred, if you wish."

"Why did th' gorilly kill th' Sidlo gur-rl instead o' carryin' her away?"

"The human mind is difficult enough to plumb; I fear I cannot look into an ape's mentality and see the thoughts he thinks, *mon vieux*. When he had stolen Mademoiselle Lefètre and borne her to the ruined chapel of the suicides the ape turned rebel. He did not go back to his cage as he was wont to do, but set out on another expedition. His small mind worked in circles. Twice he had taken women from the Shelton School, he seems to have enjoyed the pastime, so went back for more. He paused upon the roof-ledge, wondering where he should seek next for victims, and to him through the damp night air the pungent scent the Sidlo girl affected came. *Voilà*, down into the room he dropped, intent on seizing her. She was well built and strongly muscled. Also she was very frightened. She did not swoon, nor struggle in his grasp, but fought him valiantly. Perhaps she hurt him with her pointed fingernails. *En tout cas*, she angered him, and so he broke her neck in peevish anger, as a child might break its doll, and, again childlike, he flung the broken toy away.

"It was a pity, too. She was so young, so beautiful, so vital. That she should die before she knew the joys of love— *morbleu*, it saddens me. Trowbridge, my friend, can you sit there thus and see me suffer so? Refill my glass, I beg you!"